THIS WALKER BOOK BELONGS TO:

For Emma and Tiffany

First published 1996 by
Walker Books Ltd, 87 Vauxhall Walk
London SE11 5HJ

This edition published 1997

10 9 8 7 6 5 4 3 2

Text © 1996 Vivian French
Illustrations © 1996 John Prater

This book has been typeset in ITC Garamond Book.

Printed in Hong Kong

British Library Cataloguing in Publication Data
A catalogue record for this book is
available from the British Library.

ISBN 0-7445-5244-3

Once UPON A Picnic

Conceived and illustrated
by John Prater
Words by Vivian French

WALKER BOOKS
AND SUBSIDIARIES
LONDON • BOSTON • SYDNEY

Out for a picnic
Mum, Dad and me.
Not much to do.
Not much to see.

Mum is setting
up the chairs.
Here come
the three bears.

Mum and Dad
just sit and dream.
Is that a troll
beside the stream?

Nothing much
for me to do.
Who's that little girl
talking to?

Now I'm hungry
what's in here?
Biscuits, apples,
ginger beer…

That kite's high
above the ground.
What's that giant
stamping sound?

Run! Run!
As fast as you can!
Run and play
you gingerbread man!

Mr Wolf is
by the trees.
That girl's flowers
made him sneeze!

Look! A witch!
Perhaps her spell
isn't working
very well.

All those children
in that shoe.
Look how much
they have to do!

We've been sitting
here all day...
Little bear
might like to play.

Playing ball
is so much fun.
Come back, come back,
everyone!

MORE WALKER PAPERBACKS
For You to Enjoy

Also by John Prater

ONCE UPON A TIME
written by Vivian French

A little boy tells of his "dull" day, while all around a host of favourite nursery
characters act out their stories.

"The pictures are excellent, the telegraphic text perfect, the idea brilliant. We have here a classic,
I'm sure, with an author-reader bond as strong as Rosie's Walk." *Books for Keeps*

0-7445-3690-1   £4.99

THE GREATEST SHOW ON EARTH
Everyone in the circus can perform amazing feats – except, it seems, poor Harry… But there's
a twist in the tail of this entertaining big-top romp.

"John Prater's has been one of the exciting arrivals on the picture-book scene
in recent years… A wide page and bold colour push the story along with
much gusto." *The Junior Bookshelf*

0-7445-4359-2   £4.99

"NO!" SAID JOE
"A celebration of that dreaded moment when a baby first learns the intoxicating
power invested in the word 'No'. Utterly engaging fun from a gifted artist."
Jan Mark, Carousel, The Guide to Children's Books

0-7445-4718-0   £4.99